The Good Luck Horse

and other horse stories

Compiled by Vic Parker

Miles
KeLLy

First published in 2014 by Miles Kelly Publishing Ltd
Harding's Barn, Bardfield End Green, Thaxted, Essex, CM6 3PX, UK

Copyright © Miles Kelly Publishing Ltd 2014

This edition printed 2015

4 6 8 10 9 7 5 3

Publishing Director Belinda Gallagher
Creative Director Jo Cowan
Editorial Director Rosie Neave
Senior Editor Claire Philip
Designer Rob Hale
Production Elizabeth Collins, Caroline Kelly
Reprographics Stephan Davis, Jennifer Cozens, Thom Allaway
Assets Lorraine King

ISBN 978-1-78209-454-8

Printed in China

British Library Cataloguing-in-Publication Data
A catalogue record for this book is available from the British Library

ACKNOWLEDGEMENTS
The publishers would like to thank the following artists who have contributed to this book:
Advocate Art: Simon Mendez (Cover)
Beehive Illustration: Iole Rosa (main illustrations)
The Bright Agency: Kirsteen Harris-Jones (borders)

Made with paper from a sustainable forest

www.mileskelly.net
info@mileskelly.net

Contents

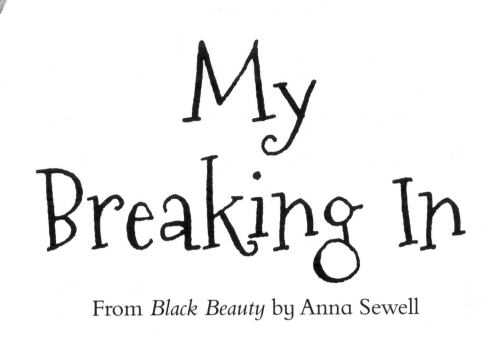

My Breaking In

From *Black Beauty* by Anna Sewell

*Anna Sewell was the first person to write a novel from
a horse's point of view. Her story is set in Victorian Britain,
and it showed how difficult a horse's life could be. The story
begins with an account of Black Beauty as a foal. He lived
on a farm with his mother and some other young horses.*

I WAS GROWING UP. My coat had become
fine and soft, and was bright black. I had
one white foot and a pretty white star on
my forehead. I was thought very handsome.

My master would not sell me till I was
four years old – he said lads ought not to

work like men and colts ought not to work
like horses till they were quite grown up.

When I was four years old, Squire
Gordon came to look at me. He examined
my eyes, my mouth and my legs. He felt
them all down, and then I had to walk and
trot and gallop before him. He seemed to
like me, and said, "When he has been well
broken in, he will do very well."

My master said he would break me in
himself, as he did not want me to be
frightened or hurt – and he lost no time
about it, for the next day he began.

Everyone may not know what breaking
in is, therefore I will describe it. It means to
teach a horse to wear a saddle and bridle,
and to carry on his back a man, woman or

child, to go just the way they wish, and to go quietly. Besides this he has to learn to have a cart fixed behind him, so that he cannot walk or trot without dragging it after him, and he must go fast or slow, just as his driver wishes.

He must never startle at what he sees, nor speak to other horses, nor bite, nor kick. He must not have any will of his own, but always do his master's will, even though he may be very tired or hungry. The worst of all is, when his harness is on, he may neither jump for joy nor lie down for weariness. So you see, this breaking in is a big thing.

I had long been used to a halter, and being led about in the fields and lanes but now I was to have a bit and bridle.

My Breaking In

That day, my master gave me some oats as usual. Then, after a good deal of coaxing, he got the bit into my mouth and the bridle fixed – but it was a nasty thing!

Those who have never had a bit in their mouths cannot think how bad it feels. A great piece of cold, hard steel as thick as a man's finger to be pushed into one's mouth, between one's teeth, and over one's tongue, with the ends coming out at the corner of your mouth, and held fast there by straps over your head, under your throat, round your nose, and under your chin, so that no way in the world can you get rid of the nasty hard thing. It is very bad! Yes, very bad! At least I thought so, but I knew my mother always wore one when she went out, and all horses did when they were grown up. And so, what with the nice oats, and what with my master's pats, kind words, and gentle ways, I got to wear my bit and bridle.

Next came the saddle, but that was not half so bad. My master put it on my back very gently, while Daniel held my head. He then made the girths fast under my body, patting and talking to me all the time.

I had a few oats, then a little leading about. And this he did every day till I began to look for the oats and the saddle. At length, one morning, my master

got on my back and rode me round the meadow on the soft grass. It certainly did feel queer, but I must say I felt rather proud to carry my master and, as he continued to ride me a little every day, I soon got used to it.

The next unpleasant business was putting on the iron shoes – that too was very hard at first. My master went with me to the smith's forge, to see that I was not hurt or frightened. The blacksmith took my feet in his hand, one after the other, and cut away some of the hoof – it did not pain me, so I stood still on three legs till he had done them all. Then he took a piece of iron the shape of my foot and clapped it on, and drove some nails through the shoe into my hoof, so that the shoe was firmly on. My feet felt very stiff and heavy, but in time I got used to it.

Having got so far, there were more new things to wear. First, a stiff heavy collar on my neck, and a bridle with great side-pieces against my eyes called blinkers – and blinkers indeed they were, for I could not see on either side – only straight in front.

Next, there was a small saddle with a nasty stiff strap that went right under my tail – that was the crupper. I hated the crupper! To have my long tail doubled up and poked through that strap was almost as bad as the bit. I never felt more like kicking, but of course I could not kick such a good master, and so in time I got used to everything and could do my work as well as my mother.

I must not forget to mention one part of my training, which was a very great help. My master sent me for a fortnight to a neighbouring farm, where there was a meadow skirted on one side by the railway. I was turned in here, among some sheep and cows.

I shall never forget the first train that ran by. I was feeding quietly near the railway fence when I heard a strange sound. It was in the distance, but before I could work out where it was coming from, there was a rush

and a clatter and a puffing out of smoke –
a long black train of something flew by and
was gone almost before I could draw my
breath. I turned and galloped to the far side
of the meadow as fast as I could go and
there I stood snorting with surprise.

During the day many other trains went by, some more slowly. These drew up at the station close by and sometimes made an awful shriek and groan before they stopped. I thought it very dreadful, but the cows went on eating quietly and hardly raised their heads as the black frightful thing came puffing and grinding past.

For the first few days I could not feed in peace, but as I found that this terrible creature never came into the field, or did me any harm, I began to disregard it, and very soon I cared as little about the passing of a train as the cows and sheep did.

Since then I have seen many horses much alarmed and startled at the sight or sound of a steam engine, but thanks to my

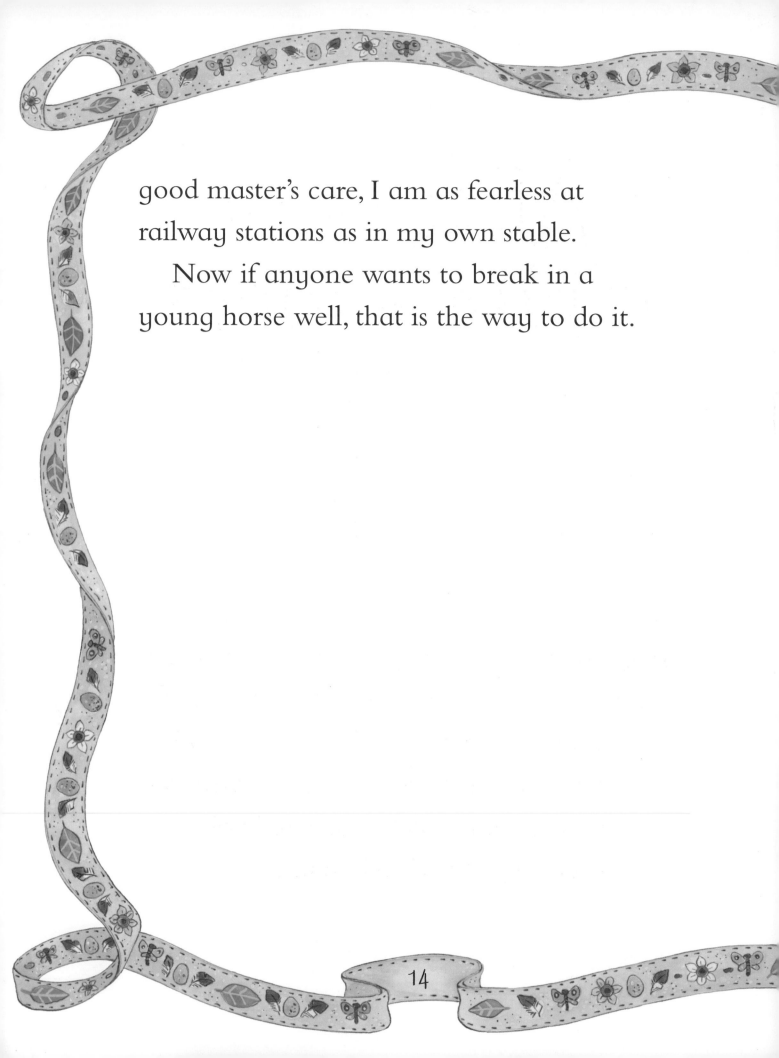

good master's care, I am as fearless at railway stations as in my own stable.

Now if anyone wants to break in a young horse well, that is the way to do it.

Alice and the White Knight

From *Through the Looking-glass* by Lewis Carroll

In this story, a young girl called Alice falls through a mirror into a back-to-front world full of chess pieces. After many magical adventures, she comes across a knight with an unusual problem…

ALICE WALKED ON IN SILENCE, every now and then stopping to help the poor knight, who certainly was not a good rider. Whenever the horse stopped, which it did very often, he fell off in front, and whenever it went on again, which it generally did rather suddenly, he fell off behind.

Otherwise he stayed on pretty well, except that he had a habit of now and then falling off sideways, and, as he generally did this on the side on which Alice was walking, she soon found that it was the best plan not to walk quite so close to the horse.

"I'm afraid you've not had much practice in riding," she ventured to say as she was helping him up after yet another tumble to the ground.

The knight looked very much surprised and a little offended at the remark. "What makes you say that?" he asked, as he scrambled back into the saddle, keeping hold of Alice's hair with one hand, to save himself from falling over on the other side.

"Because people don't fall off so often,

when they've had practice."

"I've had plenty of practice," the knight said very gravely, "plenty of practice!"

Alice could think of nothing better to say than, "Indeed?" but she said it as heartily as she could. They went on a little way in silence after this, the knight with his eyes shut, muttering to himself.

"The great art of riding," the knight suddenly began in a loud voice, waving his right arm as he spoke, "is to keep—" Here the sentence ended, as the knight fell heavily on the top of his head.

Alice was quite frightened this time and said in an anxious tone, as she picked him up, "I hope no bones are broken?"

"None to speak of," the knight said. "The

great art of riding, as I was saying, is to keep your balance properly. Like this…"

He let go of the bridle and stretched out both his arms to show Alice what he meant – and this time he fell off the horse and landed right under the horse's feet.

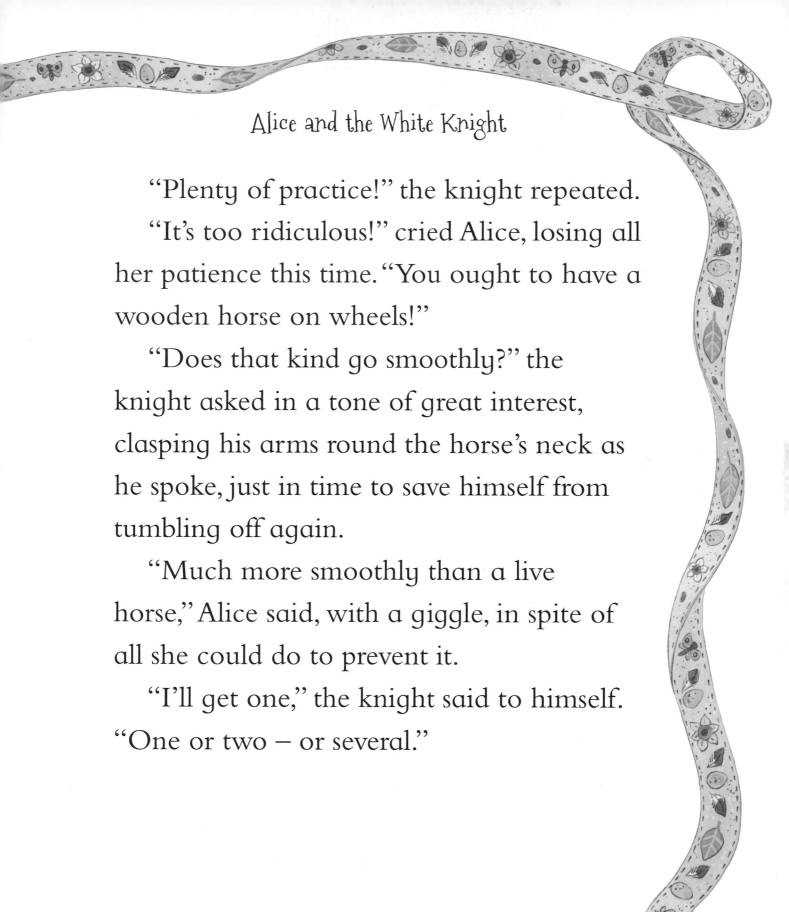

"Plenty of practice!" the knight repeated.

"It's too ridiculous!" cried Alice, losing all her patience this time. "You ought to have a wooden horse on wheels!"

"Does that kind go smoothly?" the knight asked in a tone of great interest, clasping his arms round the horse's neck as he spoke, just in time to save himself from tumbling off again.

"Much more smoothly than a live horse," Alice said, with a giggle, in spite of all she could do to prevent it.

"I'll get one," the knight said to himself. "One or two – or several."

The Ponies of the Plains

From *Long Lance* by Chief Buffalo Child Long Lance

The birth name of Chief Buffalo Child Long Lance was Sylvester Clark Long. He was an American writer, journalist and actor who lived around one hundred years ago. He was descended from Native Americans.

WITH THE FIRST TOUCH OF SPRING, we broke camp and headed south-west across the big bend of the upper River Columbia, towards the high, flat ground between the Rocky and Cascades mountains. It was here that the world's largest herd of wild horses had roamed during the last hundred and fifty years. It was these horses that we were after, to replace the herd that the storm had driven away from our camp.

We found them in early spring, after the horses had got their first good feed of green grass, and their speed had been slowed by stomach-ache.

There they were – a herd of about five hundred animals, grazing away on the side of a craggy little mountain. Their quick, alert movements, more like those of a deer than those of a horse, showed they were highly-strung beings that would dash off into space like a flock of wild birds if given the slightest cause for excitement.

There was one big, steel-dust stallion who grazed away from the rest and made frequent trips along the edge of the herd. It was obvious to our braves that this iron-coloured fellow with the silver mane was the stallion who ruled the herd.

Our warriors directed all of their attention to him, knowing that the movements of the entire herd depended on what he did. Our braves began to make little noises, so that the horses could see us in the distance, and would not be taken by surprise and frightened into a stampede. "Hoh!" our braves grunted softly.

The steel-dust stallion uttered a low whinny. All the herd raised their heads high into the air and, standing perfectly still

as though charmed, looked intently over at us with their big, nervous nostrils wide open.

They stood that way for moments, without moving a muscle, looking hard at us. Then, as we came too near, the burly stallion tried to put fear into us by dashing straight at us with a deep, rasping roar.

Others followed him, and on they came like a yelling war party, their heads swinging wildly, their racing legs wide and their long tails lashing from side to side.

Before they reached us, the speeding

animals stiffened their legs and came to a sudden halt in a cloud of dust. While they were close, they took one more good look at us, and then they turned and cantered away over the brow of the mountain.

But the big steel-dust stallion stood his ground alone for a moment and openly defied us. He dug his front feet into the dirt far out in front of him, wagged his head furiously. Around he jumped gracefully into the air, swapping ends like a dog chasing its tail. Then again he raised his head high and, with his long silver tail lying over his back, he blazed fire at us through the whites of his flint-coloured eyes. Having displayed to us his courage, his defiance and his leadership, he now turned and pranced off, with heels flying so high and lightly that one could almost imagine he was treading air.

For ten days we chased this huge family of wild horses. Then came the big night, the night that we were going to capture this great, stubborn herd. No one went to bed that evening. Shortly before nightfall, more than half of our braves quietly slipped out of our camp and disappeared.

They fanned out to the right and crept noiselessly towards the place where the herd had disappeared that afternoon. We heard wolves calling to one another. Arctic owls, night hawks and panthers were crying out mournfully in the darkness. They were our men's signals informing one another of their movements.

Then, about midnight, everything became deathly quiet. We knew that they had located the herd and surrounded it, and that they were now lying on their bellies, awaiting the first streaks of dawn and the signal to start the drive.

Next, Chief Mountain Elk went through our camp, quietly giving instructions for all hands to line themselves along a runway we had made, ready to beat in the herd. Every woman, old person, and child in the camp was called up to take part. This was important work, and everyone had to help.

The children and the women crept over to the runway and sprawled along the outside of the fence, while the men went beyond the fenced part of the runway and hid themselves behind the brush and logs, where it was a little more dangerous.

We crouched low down on the ground and shivered quietly for what felt like hours before we heard a distant, "Ho! Ho! Ho!" It was the muffled driving cry of our warriors.

For ten days they had been uttering this call to the horses to let them know that no harm could come to them from this sound, so the horses did not stampede, as they might have done if taken by surprise by a strange noise.

We youngsters lay breathless in expectancy. The thrill of the wait was almost too much! Each of us had picked out our favourite mounts in this beautiful herd of wild animals. Our fathers had all promised us that after we had caught them we could keep the ponies that we had picked, and we could hardly wait to get our hands on them.

My favourite animal was a beautiful calico pony – a roan, white and red pinto. I thought it was the best and most beautiful of the whole herd. The three different colours were splashed on his shoulders and flanks like a quilt of exquisite design.

Presently we heard the distant rumble of horses' hooves – a dull booming that shook the ground on which we lay, eagerly watching and waiting.

Then all of a sudden, "Yip-yip-yip, he-heeh-h-h!" came the night call of the wolf from many different directions. We heard the call again, "Yip-yip-yip, he-heeh-h-h!"

It was our braves signalling to one another to keep the herd on the right path.

From out of this medley of odd sounds,

we could hear the mares calling their little long-legged sons to their sides so that they might not become lost in the darkness of the night.

Our boyish hearts began to beat fast when we heard the first loud call, "Yah! Yah! Yah!" We knew straight away that action was taking place, and that the herd had now entered the runway. Our warriors were jumping up from their hiding-places and showing themselves with fierce noises, in order to stampede the horses and send them racing headlong into our camp.

Immediately there was a loud thunder of hooves. The horses were running around in great confusion. Above this din of bellowing throats and hammering feet, we heard one loud, full, deep-chested roar, which we all recognized, and it gave us boys a slight thrill of fear. It sounded like a cross between the roar of a lion and the bellow of an infuriated bull.

It was the massive steel-dust stallion, the furious king of the herd. In our imagination we could see his long silver tail thrown over his back, his legs lashing wide apart, and stark anger glistening from the whites of those incredible eyes. We wondered what he would do if he should crash through that fence into our midst.

But then, here he came, leading his raging herd, and we had no further time to think about danger. Our job was to do as the others had done all along the line – to lie still and wait until the lead stallion had passed us, and then to climb up to the top of the fence and yell and wave with all the ferocity that we could command. This was to keep the herd from crashing straight into the fence or trying to turn around, and to hasten their speed into our camp.

Therump, therump, therump! On came the loud, storming herd, *Therump, therump, therump!*

And as we youngsters peeped through the brush-covered fences, we could see their sleek backs bobbing up and down in the starlit darkness like great billows of raging water. The turbulent steel-dust stallion was leading them.

As the horses thundered closer, the steel-

grey stallion stretched himself past us like a huge greyhound.

And then a few seconds later the rest of the herd came booming past us. I thought that herd would never stop! I had never seen so many horses before, it seemed. On and on they kept coming, galloping past as if they would never stop. We soon lost count of the numbers, there were just too many! We stuck to our posts until it was nearly daylight, and still they came…

Four months later, we were again back on our beloved plains in upper Montana, and our horses were the envy of every tribe who saw us that summer.

The Good Luck Horse

An ancient Chinese folk tale

This story was first written down over two thousand years ago, by a prince called Liu An, in a book called The Huainanzi.

ONCE UPON A TIME in ancient China, there was an old man who lived near the northern border of the country. He was very poor and struggled to make a living as a farmer. But he was also very wise and was well known for having a mysterious skill – he could raise extremely fast, brave, intelligent horses.

One morning, the old man woke up to find that his favourite horse had broken out of its stall in the night and run away. He searched high and low, but could find no sign of where the stallion had gone.

The bad news spread like wildfire throughout the village, and the old man's neighbours came to see him to say how sorry they were. They expected to find the old man very downcast and upset, but to their amazement, he seemed contented. The neighbours came to comfort the old man but instead he had to reassure them!

"Do not worry yourselves," the old man told everyone. "This seems like bad luck, but it might turn out to be a blessing – you never know." The neighbours went away feeling very surprised indeed.

So the old man got on with his life quietly, without moaning once about the loss of his horse. Days, then weeks, then months went by until one day something wonderful happened.

The old farmer was out tilling his fields early in the morning when he saw an astonishing sight – his beloved stallion was approaching from the distance. And he wasn't alone, he was bringing with him a beautiful mare!

The old man gazed in disbelief for a few minutes, then he ran as fast as his aged legs could carry him to welcome back the

stallion and his new companion, and lead them safely home.

Once again, his neighbours soon came gathering to share his happiness and congratulate him. Again, they were amazed by the old man's response. Instead of finding him overjoyed, he was calm and peaceful.

"Don't get excited," the old man said. "This seems like good luck, but it might turn out to be bad thing – you never know."

The neighbours went away mumbling to themselves, shaking their heads in great confusion.

Now the old man had just one son, and he loved him very much. This son was an excellent horseman, like his father, and took it upon himself to break in and ride the newly arrived mare. As the weeks went by, the son taught the fine, wild horse to trust him, until the mare let him ride her.

But one day, disaster struck! The mare leapt a hedge and landed awkwardly, and the son fell off and broke both legs. After many months he was able to stand again, but his legs were not as they had been before. Yet the old man would not allow him to grumble. "My son," he said, "this might turn out to be a blessing."

The son did his best to be brave and bear his suffering quietly. A year later, the news came that a foreign army was attacking the northern border of China. All able-bodied young men were ordered to join the army and fight the invaders.

The old man's son saw the young men from the village go off to fight – and most did not return. However, as he was injured, he was spared. He stayed with his father and they lived for many years together.